About t

Devin Jinadasa was only 14 years old when he wrote this book. He is now a 16 year old teenager, who is studying at Asian International School in Colombo, Sri Lanka. Writing has been his passion from a young age and he has won many writing competitions in school. The only child of a director of a freight forwarding company and a lawyer, his hobbies also include drama, photography, wildlife and travelling.

Dedication

First and foremost to my mother for doing her very best for me, being a pillar of strength and support for me, at all times despite her busy work schedule. You supported me and Silver Moon Series all the way, no matter what, and were constantly nagging me to finish what I started. You believed in me throughout this journey and you are my first critique in all of my writings. The character of Aniu is based on you Amma and I hope I did you justice. You are indeed the BEST MOTHER IN THE WORLD!

To my father who the character of Lycaon is based on, for actually reading the book, something I never thought he would do and constantly supporting me with his famous grunts. You are literally a rock. Always encouraging me no matter what my choices are, just as Lycaon always supports Danny and I love you for that Thatha, thank you.

Special Thanks go to Ms. Khulsum, my former English and English Literature teacher who was one of first people to review my book. Thank you Ms K for all the support you gave me and believing in Danny. Special Thanks also goes to her mother and my Principal Mrs. Goolbai Gunasekera for supporting me and believing in this book.

To Rafil (Richie Crimson), my brother in everything but blood, there is so much I have to thank you for. For your expertise and guidance in the world of the supernatural and for all the support and help you gave me while researching vampires and hybrids. And no matter what, you will always be part of the pack.

To the real Silver Moon Wolf Pack;

Sandunika (Sandy) my Beta Female and Bhashitha (Ben) The Omega, my little brother and big sister in spirit and the first two members of the pack. Thank you for all the support that you have given me over the years. Life would never be the same without you two and I can't believe how much the three of us have done during the years since we met, including forming this pack and the bonds of friendship that have grown so strong that I consider you my own family, the brother and sister I never had. Sandunika, you have always given me the best advice when I was in trouble and always lifted my spirits in the end no matter how depressed I was. Bhashitha/Bhashi... Little Brother I have watched you grow over these years into the man you are today. You inspire me every day with your attitude and you are a pretty good sidekick.

Nikhail (Nick), my Beta and werewolf brother. Thank you so much for all that you have done for me. You inspire me when you choose not to fight other than when necessary. Your expertise on hybrids and The Wolves has been a huge help, your bone crushing hugs... not so much... but still love the hugs! Just try not to crack my ribs next time okay? Though you weren't mentioned in this book I can assure you that you'll be in the next one, little brother.

To Kawmudi my Delta female (Kelly) Thanks for being such a bright spot in my life and always making me smile, laugh and appreciate life again. Without you and your support and firm belief in me and in Danny, this book would not be half of what it is.

Last but not least my heartfelt thanks to my amazing publishers Austin Macauley Publishers Ltd. Thank so much for everything that you have done for me. I will forever be in your debt and never forget what you have done for me. Thank you so much.

Devin Jinadasa

SILVER MOON
(WAR BEGINS)

AUSTIN MACAULEY
PUBLISHERS LTD.

A CIP catalogue record for this title is available from the British Library.

ISBN 9781784554316 (paperback)
ISBN 9781784554330 (hardback)

www.austinmacauley.com

First Published (2015)
Austin Macauley Publishers Ltd.
25 Canada Square
Canary Wharf
London
E14 5LB

Printed and bound in Great Britain

Chapter 1:

I say goodbye to some old friends

One question: Do you believe in werewolves? If you're a werewolf or believe you are then **read** this, it will hopefully awaken the beast inside you, but then... the vampires will come after you and will stop at nothing to kill you. That's why you've gotta get to the Wolf House as fast as you can.

If you're a vampire then BEWARE because you'd better look behind you in exactly...10... 9... 8... 7... 6, 5, 4, 3, 2, aaaaaaa and 1! (in case you're wondering why, there's a tracking device installed on this ...Oh and don't bother looking it's well hidden and uh... oh yeah we are standing right behind you and if you've finished reading this... bye bye) . But if you're a normal kid who's reading this 'cause you think its fiction, keep right on reading too.

By the way the name's Danny. Danny McMoon and this is my story...

A few months ago, after I came home from another exhausting term at the Las Vegas Boarding school, my mom and dad (Darren and Ashley McMoon) had a surprise for me.

"California, Sonoma Valley. Danny, just think of it. A new life for us and a new school for you and..."

"What! California? Sonoma Valley? But mom, dad why do we have to move from Vegas? That means I'll have to say good bye to all my friends."

"But you can always make new ones."

"But these guys are special to me…Anyway exactly when are we leaving?"

"Oh tomorrow evening and–"

"What! We can't!"

"Daniel! We are leaving tomorrow night!" My mom's voice was dangerously angry and she looked into my dark black-brown eyes with her 'Mom Look' shining in her cat-green ones. "Isn't that right Dar…? Oh and don't even think of leaving this room, Darren McMoon." My Dad had almost gotten out the door but nothing escapes my mom's eyes. Sometimes my dad jokes that my mom has eyes at the back of her head and I seriously believe he's right.

"Can I at least go out and say good bye to them now?"

"All right but come back in for dinner," she called.

But I was already half way out the door and out into Vegas! Stopping near a couple of casinos, I ran into Scar, Kyla and Coral; three good friends of mine. They were part of my crew. They were all white girls (*I know, I know; they were white and I was Cherokee but that didn't matter to us*) and all were taller than me well except Scar. Scar whose real name was Scarlet (*but don't ever call her that unless you wanna become chopped liver)* was a caramel-haired brunette and by far one of the hottest girls I'd met. She was a thirteen year old, sassy type of girl who… and I know that this is true had rejected TWENTY guys who had asked her out. Coral was fifteen and a dark-haired brunette haired with brown eyes. Kyla was a fourteen year old blonde with blue eyes and she was a bit chubby.

"Awoooooooooooooooooooooooooooooo! Hey, T.L. Junior!" Coral let out a howl which Scarlet and Kyla echoed. (T.L. stands for Taylor Lautner. You know the actor. The dude in

'Abduction' and all those movies. The girls in my crew and well practically every girl I'd met and even some of the guys I knew had told me that I looked like a younger thirteen year old Taylor Lautner.) Plus, now I don't mean to boast but I'd been named after him since Taylor's full name is Taylor _Daniel_ Lautner.

I grinned and joined in. See I was obsessed with wolves and so was my crew.

An old guy across the street yelled at us to keep the noise down.

Then I lowered my head and gave them a hug. "Hey ladies."

"Why were you running so fast?" Scar sounded concerned.

"Well ladies I gotta tell you something... I'm leaving town."

"What? You mean just for summer right?" Kyla sounded a bit worried.

I wiped my caramel-toffee colour skinned face and ran a hand through my cropped thick jet black hair. Oh God, how was I going to explain?

Just then a greeting howl pierced the air. We turned and saw two figures striding towards us. The rest of the crew: Chris and Mark (both of them white skinned) came towards us. Chris was sixteen; a tall dude with his black hair in a fringe and ponytail. (No he's not gay) while Mark, also black-haired cut short with a side parting, was thirteen like me and Scar, but he could be a big stuck up brat when he chose to.

"Sup boss?" Chris asked me.

I know, even though I was one of the youngest in the crew, they had elected me leader. Actually it made more sense that Chris should be leader. He was the strongest. Mark was... well I could beat him in a fight at least. Since I knew the most about wolves... I guess they had elected me. I know I guess you're wondering, Reader, how I, a Cherokee Indian, had a crew of only white people. (I'm sorry if I'm being racist but it's the only way to describe them and me.) Well I was the only Native American in our neighbourhood and well me and Mark had been buds from day one of kindergarten and gradually his friends had become mine. At school, since the crew went to the same school as me, we became known as the 'Wolf Pack'.

"Danny's leaving town." Coral told them (her hands were still touching me. Coral and I were close. As in close friends but lately she'd been acting weird like taking my hand and smiling at me.)

Chris's smile broke.

"Why?" he asked looking at me.

"Parents, new life and all that crap." I said looking at him gloomily. They groaned loudly.

"Awwwwww Dan. Do you *have* to go?" Scar asked me, sadly. (Scar had been acting weird around me, too, just like Coral.)

"He he," I heard Mark scoff behind me. I whirled around.

"What is it, Mark?" I asked trying not to lose my temper.

"Well it seems pretty obvious to me," he drawled.

"Danny probably thinks he's too cool to roll with the pack now. Huh Hiawatha? Leaving to go to a better place?" He mocked me. (Did I mention that he was racist?)

I narrowly curbed my temper. So what if I was Cherokee I was proud of that fact. My ancestors originally came from Scotland but they had intermarried with Native Americans so I wasn't pure Native American, I was one sixteenth Scottish, too, but my family had been in America waaaaay longer than Mark's or anyone else's in the crew.

"If that's what you think then you're a bigger idiot than I thought." Mark took a step towards me. His hands curling into fists.

I clenched my own fists and took a defensive stance.

"Bring it." I raised my fists.

He threw his fist in swinging punch. I got ready to duck but before I could do that Chris's hand shot out to grab Mark's arm.

"Don't be stupid." Kyla told Mark. "Danny doesn't wanna go any more than we want him to go. Now stop acting like a spoiled brat." (She'd been acting weird too.)

Mark pulled his arm back, looked at her, then me.

"Whatever, losers," he said digging his hands into his jeans as he strode off angrily into the darkness.

But not before I had seen tears rolling down his face. I could tell the dude would miss me. He and I had grown up together after all, even if he was a jerk sometimes.

"Bye... Mark..." I whispered. Then my cell phone beeped. It was a text from my mom.

Dinner's ready. Come home NOW! We have 2 pack after we eat. So hurry!

"Oh man, sorry guys I gotta go."

"Do you have to?" Coral asked.

"Sorry guys but I gotta go... Hasta la vista." I said giving Chris a high five. He clenched my fist then gave me a pat on the back. I nodded to him.

"See ya bro."

Then I turned to the girls. I held out my hand for a high five...

"Oh screw that!" Coral, Kyla and Scar yelled together in a union. They grabbed me in a hug. My face seemed really warm since they had never hugged me like this before and I could've sworn Coral and Kyla were crying.

We stayed like that for a minute while Chris looked over their shoulders grinning at me. Then we pulled apart. I felt a bit weak in the knees and a bit dizzy but I waved one hand and turned to go.

"I'll miss you D-Wolf," Coral whispered in my ear.

"More than you'll ever know or understand..." Scar whispered in my other ear. Then she leaned in and gave me a kiss on the cheek.

"Good bye Danny... We'll miss you," Kyla said, our faces inches apart. Then I turned and headed back home...

Chapter 2:

I'm a lean mean Sonny Rango beating machine

So here I am (dressed in blue jeans and a grey T-shirt) Standing in front of the Sonoma Valley High School. I can describe it to you, and yep it'll probably be the same as your own school. Huge walls, big front door, corridors and class rooms, kids running around yelling... Sound familiar? Yeah. Anyway I found my class and walked in just as the bell rang.

"Class, we have new student this semester." Said Ms. Millie Pandora. "This is Daniel McMoon. So I want you all to make him feel welcome."

The kids looked at me, sizing me up.

"Now Danny why don't you just sit there next to... Gwen De La Rosa." She said pointing to a cute girl wearing a red T-shirt and jeans: a slender brown-eyed beauty with black or light brownish hair it was hard to tell, with the long well-muscled legs and tanned skin of an athlete, she looked about my age (but I found out later that she was really twelve). She was a couple of inches taller than me (Talk about genes huh?) and looked a whole lot more athletic at the back of the class A typical Californian beauty but in my eyes _way_ hotter. Nice, no wait scratch that... AWESOME! Except for the 'couple of inches taller' part. So I walked up to her and even though it was only like three rows away, it seemed like three thousand miles with all the kids staring at me, but the girl I was gonna sit next to, totally ignored me. I sat down next to her just as Pandora turned around and started explaining about the world pollution... Or something.

"Hi there, name's Danny." She looked at me as if I was a dork.

"I know who you are. Pandora just told us."

"Oh... yeah, right." I tried to get her attention again.

"So how long have you been here?"

Instead of answering me she just looked down at her book.

"Ooooookay, not a bad start," I thought as the bell sounded.

Kids piled into the doorway so naturally I was the last to leave. Just as I walked out I felt a tap on my shoulder.

"Hey there. You're the new dude right?" I turned and saw a guy standing behind me.

"Yeah," I replied while sizing the guy up. He was about a head taller than me with curly black hair and pure black eyes.

The guy threw out his palm for a high five.

"Richie Crimson."

I slapped it but the moment his hand touched mine, my fingers nearly broke!

I tried to say something but in truth the only thing that came into my mind was "AAAAAAAAAAhhhhhhhh!"

I managed to squeak out my name and would have said more if I hadn't seen a girl standing behind Richie. Three letters came into my mind 'H-O-T'. The girl was a blonde and had eyes that seem to flash different colors every time the light caught it, with skin so pale it looked almost snow white.

Richie caught me looking and said "Oh booooy. Looks like someone's fallen for Karen Blood... Again!"

I shook my head and turned to Richie and was in the middle of saying "No way, man." but stopped when I saw his expression. Richie's face was tightened with anger and rage, but the moment he saw me looking, his face cleared and returned to his old smile

"Oh. Uh sorry, Danny, but I err... gotta run."

And with that he dashed around the corner. Something strange was going on...

An eternity of torture later...

"Danny and Karen sitting in a tree. K-I-S-S-I-N-G..."

Shane started singing again and by the way, he's a terrible singer, so I covered my ears and dropped my head onto the lunch table trying to block out the sound but no luck, Shane's voice rang out loud and clear.

"Shane, buddy, c'mon drop it all right, so I like her a little, it's no big deal... you don't have to broadcast it to the whole world, you know." I groaned covering my ears and banging my head on the cafeteria table.

Richie had introduced me to a couple of friends at the cafeteria: Shane Wilson was younger than me by a year and an African American and about the same height as me with brown eyes with black hair combed sideways on his forehead. Chuck Anderson was the hugest guy I'd ever seen. He was an African American who looked literally like a huge brown bear without hair with huge beefy arms that looked like they could easily lift up thousand pound weights plus again he was younger than me (Un-freaking-believable! How come almost all the people who are younger than me are my height or taller?). He had short black hair like a buzz cut, wore glasses and was a bit chubby. Ted and Sam Jackson were Native American brothers (like me) but Ted was my age and had darker skin while Sam was younger at twelve. He was the fairest of us and wore glasses. Both of them were black haired with the same milk chocolate eyes. They came from the Pomo tribe while I came from the Cherokee Tribe.

But reader even though we were from different Tribes we belonged to the same Clan. We Native Americans formed secret Clans made up of people from different tribes and even some of the white men to keep peace within the tribes and white men. Each Clan took an animal as their symbol and name. Apparently they had been born into the Wolf Clan like me.

The two Beckets were Sandy who was another Native American (Cherokee and Wolf Clan) who was about Richie's height with chocolate brown skin, brown eyes and curly black hair tied in a short black braid, and Ben who was the youngest in our group at eleven, he had the same complexion as his sister and by the way is NOT related to Ben 10; Kelly Drago who was yet another Native American this time from the Inuit Tribe, also of the Wolf Clan had brown skin and long black hair which she tied in a ponytail that went down past her shoulders. She had deep chocolate brown eyes. Finally Lee Rodriguez, who was the tallest of us and skinny with pale skin and had short curly black hair,

"Yeah I guess..." He paused for a second then broke into a huge grin "but I just love to annoy you." I gave him a light punch on the shoulder.

"Danny and me?" asked a new voice behind me and I nearly died on the spot. There leaning against the back of my chair was... Karen herself!

"Yeah," Ted began.

"And that's because he –Mmmmmmmm!"

Yeah and that part's because I clamped a hand over his big, fat, hippo-sized... no scratch that... Blue Whale-sized hole of a mouth to stop him spilling the beans.

"Yeah, Karen, um I wanted you to be my... um... my...Lab partner!" I said (I know, I know. Lame excuse, but hey, I was panicking here!) While I gave my deluxe 'you're dead meat' stare to Richie and the others.

"Hmm, all right Da – what's your name again."

"Danny."

"All right Danny," and with that she left.

I was so relieved that I barely noticed that I was choking Ted until he yelled so loud I bet my old crew could hear us back in Vegas!

"Oh, sorry man." I released Ted and he quickly gulped down air.

"Geez, Dan, it was only a laugh."

"I know but –"

Just then the bell rang and everyone headed for the gym.

"Okay guys, today's wrestling day so today's paringsare..." Coach Mike looked over us.

"Danny versus Sonny."

Sonny Rango was naturally one of the school bullies, which was hilarious since he was the shortest kid in the grade. If you want a description just remember that saying 'a lean, mean, fighting machine' cause that's exactly what he was! He would have been handsome once......if his face (which was covered in bruises and one black eye) didn't look like an ugly squashed tomato. He grinned at me and cracked his knuckles. Did I mention that he wanted to kill me because I had been looking at Karen who naturally was his girlfriend.

He grinned menacingly and whispered "You're dead, newbie."

"And ready... Fight!" yelled Coach and Rango ran towards me with a roar of rage. But I did the thing people do naturally in this kind of situation: I RAN! Rango chased after me yelling and cursing while the others booed. Then suddenly I was tripped by one of Rango's pals and fell hard on my shoulder.

Sonny came up and looking down at me he smiled and said, "You can't run now can you, newbie." He kicked me hard in the stomach and for a second I couldn't breathe!

Coach immediately ran over and said "Hey, hey, Sonny I told you – No KICKING!"

Sonny sniggered and said "Okay, Coach." Which meant he wasn't a bit sorry then he turned back to me, grabbed my neck and lifted me up, but I wasn't going to be so easy to take down now because when he had kicked me, something inside me had awakened and I felt so angry like I could take on a thousand Sonny Rangos and turn them all into barbecued shish kebabs! Extra crispy!

Sonny pulled his fist back to punch me in the face but I reached out and grabbed his hand and twisted it. He dropped me with a gasp but as soon as he let go I was on the attack, I punched him twice in the stomach, then held him in a headlock while he tried to pulverize my stomach but I was so mad I didn't feel a thing. One of Rango's pals grabbed me and flung me back onto the ground. I jumped straight back up and grabbed Rango's neck and choke-slammed him onto the ground hard, onto his back and then prepared to deliver the final blow but then Coach came and grabbed me and said

"Um okay, Danny… Easy now, that's enough."

I turned towards Coach and nearly attacked him, too, but that sudden burst of anger was gone and I felt weak and exhausted like I had fought a hundred people at the same time. Sonny lay on the floor whimpering like a baby, his face slowly turning back from blue to normal. I looked at Gwen and her face was a mask; I couldn't tell whether she was frightened or amazed but when I looked at Karen she looked amused. Then I caught the gang's eyes and all of them looked amazed and excited and a little scared too.

Then coach announced that for the second round that I would be facing Gwen.

"Ha this'll be a piece of cake."

I figured, as I was feeling pretty good after my victory over Rango, that I'd just knock Gwen to the ground without actually hurting her since I never hit girls. So I smiled at Gwen and to my surprise she actually smiled back... Right before she tripped me up, flipped me in mid-air, onto my back and sat on top of me before I even realized what was happening. Then she leaned in until she was right next to my ear and said

"One piece of advice Danny, never underestimate a girl."

"Um... okay... but can you please get off me first?" I groaned.

Gwen was heavier than she looked. But even after she got off I was still on my back groaning. Finally Richie came over and helped me up and I could tell he was trying not to laugh.

"Oh yeah I forgot to tell you, Gwen has beaten everybody she's faced... so sorry."

"Oh you *forgot*?!" I asked through clenched teeth. "Man, she nearly broke every bone in my body!"

"Sorry, but don't worry, it'll wear off in a couple hours, or was it days? I forgot, was it days... or hours... Or weeks... or months or..."

"Never mind, forget it!" I cried. Knowing Richie, he could go on for hours. Thankfully Coach announced that for the third round it was Gwen versus... Karen.

"Ooh, cat fight, this is going to be good," I heard Shane mutter, standing next to me, just as Gwen landed the first blow hard, but Karen dodged with amazing speed and countered. I had never seen a fight like this ever in my entire thirteen and a half years of life. They were fighting so hard they seemed like blurs and I could see that each face was burning with anger.

Finally Coach said, "All right girls break it up, that's enough for today." But even though both stopped, I could still see the hatred and anger burnt into their faces and sensed their reluctance to stop the fight plus Gwen was shaking so much it looked like she was either about to barf or tear us all apart.

Karen flounced off to change but Gwen came up to us with her friends Trisha Gomez and Diana Nathan and said:

"Hey, guys."

"Hey, Gwen." the others replied. (*I didn't know they knew her*)

"Sorry… almost lost control."

"Hey don't worry. We all lose control sometimes."

"Whoa, whoa! You guys know her and you never told me!"

"Oh sorry, Danny, but… um… are you coming to the party tonight?" asked Ben, lamely.

"What party?" I asked.

"Karen Blood's."

"OF COURSE!" I yelled.

"Okay, party's tonight at eight."

"Okay where do I meet you guys?"

"At the old bus stop down the road five minutes from school it's about ten minutes to Blood's house from there," said Sandy.

Chapter 3:

Wolves give me a history lesson

That evening, after a quick shower and changing into jeans, a pure black T-shirt and my Adidas sneakers, I looked in the mirror of the tiny room I'd been given in a tiny house about the size of my old sitting room. This was totally lame compared to my condo in Vegas. A guy with black hair cropped short, toffee-coloured tanned skin and dark brown eyes stared back at me. Man tonight... Even *I* admitted that I did look a little like Taylor Lautner.

Ten minutes later I met up with the others (except for Gwen and her friends, which to my surprise was a little disappointing) at the old bus stop, like ten minutes from Karen's house, as Sandy had said.

We dashed around the corner and arrived at a large ranch-style house. Inside kids were dancing to the tune of 'Go Ahead' by DJ Khaled playing on the DJ set.

"Hey guys I'll go get drinks," I called over my shoulder and headed for the drink stand.

"Sure but meet us back here in five minutes okay," called Shane.

"Okay," I called back over my shoulder.

I got the drinks and was about to head back when I felt a hand on my shoulder and a soft voice in my ear saying

"Hey, Danny." It was Karen.

"Uh hey, Karen! Happy Birthday!"

"Danny, can you come in here for a moment?"

She pointed to a small basement.

"Um… Sure." We headed down the stairs and came into a small room. As soon as I entered the room, she immediately locked the door, turned to me, walked over slowly and said:

"Daniel McMoon… did you really think I wouldn't know."(*How did she know my surname?*)

"Huh?"

"I knew there was something about you the moment I saw you." I gulped since I'd never been *alone* in a room with a girl before… definitely not with a super model like Karen…

"What something? I don't stink do I?"

"Oh you don't have to pretend. After that fight with my boyfriend only an idiot wouldn't know what you are."

"Uh exactly what are you talking about…?"

She stepped in real close (our faces inches apart) and said "Danny I feel really bad about this but unfortunately…"

She looked so beautiful: she was wearing a red dress and her blood red eyes were glowing and her razor sharp fangs were gleaming… Wait... Red eyes… fangs… FANGS!

"WHOA!"

I jumped sideways just before her teeth closed around the place where my throat had been a second ago.

She hissed and turned towards me again.

"Karen… You're a… .a –" I stuttered.

Karen smiled through her fangs.

"Vampire?"

She laughed. "Of course, Danny. Who else would want a young werewolf dead?"

"Wait! You called me a young what?"

But before I could blink she had her hand around my neck and raised her other hand which had clawed finger nails, to slice me to pieces!

Then the wall burst open and out of the smoke stepped a pack of wolves. That's right: Wolves! But these Wolves were huge; their heads came right up to my chest!

One Wolf, a beautiful pure white female, with long lustrous sleek fur, came up to me and sniffed me and looked at me with warm brown eyes that looked strangely familiar, but I was too worried about being turned into wolf chow. "Great. Now I'm going to become a chew toy for these guys as well as torn to pieces by her." I thought looking at the-thing-that-used-to-be-Karen who looked… afraid? Why would a vampire be afraid of wolves? Sure these wolves were bigger than most wolves but…?

The white Wolf turned to her and growled so did the other wolves.

"You!" Cried Karen and ran for the stairs but seven of the strange Wolves blocked her way: a golden sand brown wolf, a dark silver wolf, a massive brown wolf that was like biggest of them all with black oval markings around its eyes, a chocolate brown and a grey and a light grey blocked the way.

The other wolves closed in: the white Wolf flanked by a big dark brown, a smaller silver Wolf with two odd circles around its eyes alongside a brown Wolf with the same odd dark circles around its eyes and a dark grey Wolf closed the circle around Karen.

The white wolf rushed forward snarling but Karen shoved it hard and the white wolf fell hard on its side. Karen immediately dashed forward at lightning speed jumped through the wolf shaped hole in the wall and was gone before anyone noticed.

The white she-wolf got back on its feet and rushed to the opening with half of the pack with it but they soon came back and then of course they had to notice me. The white wolf sniffed me again then it… it…stood up on its hind legs and… changed… into… Gwen.. GWEN! (Normal old Gwen in a white T-shirt and dark blue jeans in which she looked amazing.)

She looked at me and said "You all right?" and then without waiting for an answer she turned back to the wolves

"Alright guys you can phase now."

The Wolves changed just like Gwen: the golden sand brown wolf turned into Sandy, the dark silver into Richie, the huge brown wolf turned into Chuck, the chocolate brown turned into Lee, the grey turned into Shane, the light grey turned into Ben. The dark brown turned into Trisha, the wolves with the weird circles turned into Sam and Diana and the dark grey wolf turned into Ted!

"What the heck! My friends are Wolves! I can't believe it!"

"Now Danny, calm down," said Sandy.

"Calm! I'm perfectly calm… Just tell me how a guy can be friggin' calm when his friggin' friends just happen to be FRIGGIN' WOLVES!"

"Uh, Danny, we are actually WEREWOLVES not ordinary wolves. We call ourselves Wolves with a capital W so it's easier," said Ben.

"Benjamin Becket! Now he'll just freak out more!" chided Sandy.

I'd love to say that I took this very calmly but the truth is I did freak out more.

"You mean you guys are… FREAKING BIG, MONSTER, PEOPLE-KILLING WOLVES?!"

At this, Gwen grabbed me and slammed me against the wall (Great – now I was sure Gwen would kill me if she kept this up).

"Danny! We are NOT killers okay; we protect people from Blood suckers like your friend who tried to kill you just now. That's what we were created to do: Protect. And now, Danny, I'm sorry, but we have to knock you out now. Sorry." And that's the last I remembered after I felt a crashing blow on my head that I later learnt was from Richie, the slimy weasel.

When I came around I found myself lying in cave on a bed of sand. The cave seemed oddly familiar like I had been there before but I'd never been to this place at all. I got up, dusted off the unfamiliar black shorts and white T-shirt and turned... right into the eyes of a huge white she-Wolf with silver eyes like miniature moons. I mean I knew she couldn't talk but when I looked at her...I... could understand her... like I could read her movements...

"Aaaaah! Where am I?"

I asked edging as far away from those sharp teeth as possible as I had no intention of being dinner for the Wolf.

Greetings, my young cub. Do you not recognize the place where you were born?– The wolf sighed – *Ah it has been many moons since I looked upon your face. As for where you are, you are at the house of your ancestors, the house of Wolf! The home that one of your elder brothers, Jack London, built for us as a sanctuary and a headquarters: The Wolf House* (Yeah The Wolf House, Sonoma Valley. How I got there... I have no idea!)

"Whaaaaa! How the hell can you talk!?"

Apologies, I did not mean to frighten you but since you are my cub I expected you to be used to this as all Wolves have this ability

"You mean the ability to talk to giant Wolves? I'm going crazy!"

No you are not crazy. It is their fault! I expected the two I entrusted you to would have sent you earlier to me for training.

"Whoa, whoa, what training? And who are you?"

The training you were going to receive was to toughen yourself for battle as all werewolves do against the Cold Ones.

"Wait a sec, first of all I'm not a werewolf, I'm just an ordinary kid with ordinary problems and who are the 'Cold Ones'?"

The 'Cold Ones' are another name for the creatures you call vampires such as the one that tried to kill you. As for who I am well... I was known as Lupa (Loo-pa) to the Romans: the she-wolf that raised the founder of Rome and his twin brother: Romulus and Remus your two elder brothers who were among the first male werewolves to walk this land; they were strong, loyal, brave and defended each other with their lives and it was a shame that Romulus had to kill his brother as he had become a hybrid...

"Hey you mean he could transform into a car? That's so cool! Are all werewolves like that? Can I turn into a Lamborghini?" (Weird I'd never heard about werewolves turning into cars, but then I'd never known werewolves existed in the first place.)

The she-wolf smiled; *Hmm ha, ha aha, no, my young cub, I meant that darkness had filled his heart and turned him into a Cold One as well as a Wolf like a cross between a dog and a cat I suppose. He had become the creature that these new TV shows show: the half man, half wolf creature but they do not realize that the man part is actually the vampire part of the creature and the foolish humans believe that we the werewolves look like that!*

The she-Wolf gave a sudden snarl that made me jump. Then she licked her chest fur.

But back to my story Romulus loved his brother and hated to kill him but he had to for the sake of his pack and the people of Rome, but it was a fierce fight and struggle before Remus was defeated. Romulus won only because he had faith and called upon the power of his father, Mars, and the Moon's. But even though Remus was evil he was good once and I still love him and Romulus but enough of that.

"How is that possible? I mean how can he... like become a hybrid?"

I don't know, Daniel... I think it's best if I tell you later...

I was also known as Moro (Mau-ro) to the Japanese: The great giant two tailed wolf goddess who also raised the first She-werewolf: a girl by the name of San who led the forest gods of the Boars and Wolves against the humans who were cutting down the trees of their forest home and even though the battle was lost she taught the Japanese people to respect the forest and its other inhabitants.

The people of Turkey held me in the same regard as the Romans did as I was known to them as Ashiai Tuwu the mother of the first great Khans. I was also called Asena. I rescued an injured boy, nursed him back to health, and then bore him ten half-wolf half-human children. The eldest of these, Bumin Khayan, became chieftain of the Turkic tribes.

I was known to the people of India as Raksha (Ra-k-sha) the wolf mother of Mowgli the Man cub who I am sure you know as there were famous tales about his adventures. Many I am sure you have heard of. I am known by a lot of other names and stories around the world some that go back to the dawn of the humans but it will take too long so I will just tell you the name I was most commonly known as here in America... it is Aniu (Aa-na-u)... And I am your mother and Lycaon (Ly-can) the First Werewolf and Alpha of the First Wolf Pack is your father...

You know after a night of friends turning into wolves and vampires trying to kill me you'd think I'd have no problem handling this right? Well... your absolutely, positively... WRONG!

"Um... Aniu... Err you're not my mom, my mom's Ashley McMoon and my dad is Darren McMoon, and..."

But at that moment a giant black Wolf with amber eyes came into the cave. It was bigger than Aniu and that's saying a lot because Aniu was the size of fully grown grizzly bear, but this black Wolf was at least a head taller.

*Lycaon...*Aniu nodded to the black wolf and licked its muzzle.

Aniu is this him? An amber gaze found my eyes.

Yes Lycaon this is him, our son.

"Whoa, whoa, I am NOT your son! I'm just a normal teenager with normal problems."

Daniel, you are our son and the true born leader of the Silver Moon Wolf Pack. Aniu gazed at me with sympathetic eyes and said *I am sorry that you had to wait so long to find out but...*

"Look I'm not a leader okay, I'm a loser, and when you say Lycaon do you mean *the* Lycaon, the one in Greek mythology. The king that Zeus turned into a wolf guy?"

Yes I was the first werewolf. The king that Zeus turned into a wolf. He slew my fine fifty other sons with his lightning bolts and sent me to haunt the lonely mountains. Lycaon growled fiercely(Yeah I know what you're thinking imagine having *FIFTY* half-brothers! I mean having one is well okay...ish by me, hell even two but *FIFTY* now that was...well bit... too much and that was just by one parent!*)*

"So..." I asked, "Shouldn't you be... I don't know a ... guy?"

Lycaon growled. *Yes I am a man as well as a Wolf but I prefer to stay in my animal form... But I suppose you should know what I look like as a human.*

Then he reared onto his hind legs just like Gwen and the others and changed into a really buff guy who looked about forty five with his short black hair almost a buzz cut (I could tell he was going bald) and a prickly beard who looked a lot like me: the same shoulders, nose and his hair...well what was left of it looked exactly like mine. He grinned then changed back into the giant black wolf.

At first I was angry and took out my anger out on the humans by killing them as revenge for the loss of my sons. Then I met Aniu and we fell in love and she became my mate. And she tried to lessen my anger towards the humans but then I met the worst enemy I had ever faced: Count Dracul known as Dracula to you. At first he and I became friendly with each other; we became 'partners' I suppose. He helped me take my revenge on the humans and promised that he would help me regain my old kingdom and for a time, together we were invincible...

Then he betrayed me because he wanted to take over my former Greek kingdom of Arcadia for himself unlike our previous agreement. Aniu and I challenged him over and over again in many places and he tried to kill Aniu but I had already lost so many that I cared about, I was not going to lose Aniu as well! (Aniu licked him at this)*I attacked him with all the anger and strength I could summon in the city of London and set him on fire but even while he was set on fire he fought and that fire caused the Great Fire of London but these foolish mortal humans thought it was started by a HUMAN! Dracul fought on until the sun rose and I pinned him to the ground and he met his end in my jaws...*

(Wow! Now that was pretty cool.)

Zeus saw the battle and was so touched that I had changed so much that he allowed my other fifty sons to return from the dead, and he also told me that Dracul was not the last enemy I would face so he told me to create a pack of creatures just like Aniu and myself to defend Mankind and so the first Wolf Pack was formed by myself, Aniu, our friends who were granted immortality and Zeus made Aniu and I immortal so that forevermore Aniu and I would be there to counsel young werewolves such as yourself and prepare them for battle against the Cold Ones even after the gods themselves faded away...; so now do you believe that we are your mother and father?

"Well...No! You guys are not my parents, Darren and Ashley are."

Which is where you are wrong, boy! Lycaon growled. *Are these the 'parents' you were looking for?*

With that he walked out but returned dragging.... my parents or fake parents or whatever...I ran to them.

"Mom, Dad... are you okay?"

"Daniel. Are you alright?" asked Mom, or fake Mom.

"Yeah but –"

Why doesn't he know! growled Lycaon.

"Lycaon!" Aniu whined. *"These humans looked after our cub all these years for us. They showed him love and patience and for that reason treat theses humans well... please Lycaon..."*

Ashley turned to Aniu and nodded her head and bowed. Aniu inclined her head warmly in return.

But my Dad or Darren faced Lycaon and said "When you gave him to us, we didn't want a freak we wanted a normal son."

Don't talk about my son like that! Aniu who a second ago was calm and full of gratitude, seemed moments away from ripping out Darren's throat after hearing Darren's remark.

"Wait a minute; I'm not your son?" I felt my jaw drop.

Fake Mom or Ashley faced me and said, "Danny I'm sorry... I still love you as if you were my own son but... Aniu is right... I'm so sorry, Danny."

I felt like someone had torn me apart, I mean how many of you, readers have found out that the 'parents' that supposedly looked after you for thirteen and a half years are not your real family at all!

Aniu nuzzled me and snarled at Ashley and Darren *Go away from here and never return...*

They left without a word and never looked back.

Aniu turned to me and said ***Daniel... Go outside... We need to talk...***

Chapter 4:

Richie becomes a tour guide

I immediately scrammed for the exit. When I came out of the cave I found myself in a large supersized stone and redwood mansion with an Olympic-sized swimming pool, a stone floor and statues of wolves in every pose. A huge staircase led up to the top of the house. Then I spotted Richie coming towards me with the rest of the crew...no *pack*.

"Hey Danny! Welcome to the pack of the Silver Moon." He put his head back and gave an exaggerated howl. The others swarmed around me.

"So Danny, how are you feeling?" asked Lee. His voice was concerned.

"Um how about extremely confused... uh... frightened and feeling like I've gone... FREAKING CRAZY," I replied.

He laughed. "Hey don't worry, you'll get used to it."

I looked around and saw Gwen leaning against a pillar near the pool with her arms folded. Trisha and Diana flanked her. I pushed my way to her then said:

"You knew all along that I was a werewolf didn't you?"

She frowned and said "Honestly, Danny... No. All we knew was that someone who was one of us was going to arrive and that someone would be pretty powerful against those *LEECHES!"*

She said that last word with a look of disgust and all of the others had similar looks on their faces.

"Hey... um... guys I don't want to put your hopes up for nothing so I'll just lay it on you flat... I don't have a SINGLE CLUE about being a werewolf."

"Hey don't worry, with the way we are going to train you... Well, by the next full moon you'll be a lean mean vampire killing Machine!" Sam cried.

"Oh joy..." I muttered.

Gwen cleared her throat and everyone immediately looked at her.

"Okay since Danny's the newest member of the pack, that means Richie is no longer the Omega and since he is the newest pack member he gets the tour guide job unless Danny is... No he can't be."

She shook her head dismissively.

"Anyway Shane, take Chuck, Ted, Sam and Lee. The five of you can cover the Nevada border. The rest of us will stay here."

"Right." The group on patrol changed into wolf form and dashed away at literally, the speed of Light.

"Okay, C'mon Danny lets show you around eh?" Richie called leading the way outside.

Richie showed me all around the Wolf House. There was a basketball court and an obstacle course, there was a track for running and an actual racecourse, but Richie didn't say what it was for, there was a pit where Richie said practice fights were held and he also showed me a large baseball diamond and a small soccer field.

We came to a grassy meadow which had redwood trees bordering it and climbed a small hill.

"So... Richie..."I panted as we climbed the slippery slope, "... How in the world do werewolves exist? I thought they were myths, you know scary stories to frighten us when we were kids."

Richie laughed. "I know how you're feeling Danny, but you heard Lycaon's story didn't you? We exist because vampires exist. We are kind of like their bane. You know, the only thing that can kill them and protect the humans I guess."

"So what's it like being a... a Wolf?"

I asked as we reached the top of the hill, from there I could see the entire Wolf House. It looked like a cross between a log cabin and a billionaire's mansion and shaped in a giant U.

Richie lay down on the grass with his hands behind his head while I sat down beside him. Then he said:

"Well I guess it's pretty cool... I mean when you're a Wolf you can run faster than anything, even a vampire. Oh yeah and we are like super strong, you know... even Ben who's the youngest member of the pack can move a ten ton boulder with one hand. Plus we can hear, see, and smell things better than any living thing on the planet!"

"And we don't need the full moon or anything, right?"

He laughed "That old legend? Nope. But the full moon does have a connection to us. See a Wolf on a normal day is pretty powerful on its own but on the day of the full moon our power is double what it is now and on the day of the full moon you feel... like you can do anything at all! No matter how impossible!"

"So Rich, are we the only werewolf pack in the world?" I asked still trying to grasp what this all meant.

"Oh hell no, Danny!"

His head shot up.

"There are hundreds of packs out there, course we never talk to them but we know they're out there and well we keep a distance..."

"So… How many packs are here in America right now?"

"Um well we're there of course… but there's also …*Fenrir's Blood Moon Pack* in Arkansas whom we know of."

Richie said trying to disguise the hate in his voice. "But now more and more humans are turning into vampires, thanks to the increase in the *Leech* population. So we're not exactly sure."

"Who's Fenrir?" I asked.

"Oh I forgot you didn't know. See Lycaon and Fenrir are brothers. Fenrir became a werewolf after he tried to avenge Lycaon's punishment. He, too, hated the humans but he became good in the end… at least a while ago. The Inuits of Alaska called him Amarok. Amarok was a lone wolf, and did not travel with a pack. He was known for preying upon hunters foolish enough to go out at night. According to legend, Amarok came to the people when the caribou became so plentiful that the herd began to weaken and fall sick. Amarok came to prey upon the frail and ill caribou, allowing the herd to become healthy once more, so that man could hunt. But he recently in the last two centuries formed his own pack in Arkansas after he left Alaska."

"Huh I didn't know that." I asked surprised "So I have an *UNCLE* who's a Wolf, too! Isn't there anyone who I know who isn't a Wolf?!"

Richie laughed. "Well, pretty much… NO!"

"Oh ha, ha, ha, real funny, Rich," I laughed, sarcastically.

"So anyway what's the problem?"

"Well… Lycaon and Fenrir kinda had a fight recently… And uh… well Fenrir turned evil and now he works with the bloodsuckers. We heard rumours about an attack any day now and his pack outnumbers us three to one, plus he's got those *Leeches* on his side. That's why we need all the new pack members we can get."

"Oh…" I said in a small voice. Great… Just great. I'm a werewolf and now I'm going to die… wonderful.

Richie noticed and said "Hey c'mon buddy, you never know… We might even win." He grinned.

I grinned feebly. Leave it to Richie to cheer me up.

"Richie what are the ranks in the pack?"

"Huh?" Richie looked confused.

"I mean remember Gwen called me an Omega and said that now you were promoted or something."

Richie grinned "Oh yeah that. Well any wolf or werewolf pack has ranking members, kind of like a king and his court. In our pack…

"Well there's the Alpha, the head of the pack, the big cheese, the leaders]. The Alpha eats first, kills first and leads the pack into battle and all. We have to follow the Alpha's orders whether we want to or not.

"Then there's the Beta Male and Female who are second in command and takes over the pack if the Alpha dies. After them are the Deltas. The Deltas are wolves in training for Beta position. They are third in rank to Alpha and Beta. Deltas do not hold the authority to call medium or large Hunts. That is a privilege to only ranked Alphas, Betas, and Hunters. Deltas usually become the next Beta after training is complete but one can remain Delta without moving to Beta position. When this is the case, if ever the current Beta is removed from their rank, steps down, changes rank, or leaves the pack, the Delta may take the place as the new Beta at the Alpha's request. Until then they gives orders on the Alphas' behalf if the Alphasare sick or something and like the Alphas we have to obey the Betas' and Deltas' orders too.

"Then after them is the rest of the pack which I was recently promoted to. Since we are the cubs who make up the rest of the pack, we aren't exactly real pack members yet, at least not until our first hunt, but after we turn fourteen and go from cub to a full adult member of the Pack; we get our ranks, such as:

"Sentinels; their job is to ensure that the pack is safe by patrolling the territory and watching the movements of the surroundings. They are to make sure that no intruders enter the clearing. In doing so, it is a Sentinel's responsibility to greet new visitors and learn why they are here and where they come from. Being in that position, it is the Sentinel's job to make sure each new visitor that comes into the clearing has good intentions as well. When the Sentinel is not present within the meeting or if there is none, the greeting responsibilities go to all Adult Pack members. Sentinels also make sure that the Pack Members keep themselves out of trouble, and that no fights break out between visiting wolves (or other pack members), warning them of the rules. After the warning, the Sentinel reserves the right to kick a continually aggressive or provoking wolf out of the channel and set a temporary ban. If this does happen the Sentinels are to report to their Alpha and/or Beta and tell them what happened.

"Hunters. The Hunters are those wolves who are exceptionally skilled at tracking and hunting down prey. They can range from large or small, but it is mainly their skill as a Hunter that counts. The Hunters make sure that the Pack has a full abundance of food. After large hunts, the lead Hunter will memo with an update of the food available. Hunters lead the hunts along with the Alpha and/or Beta, directing the members on when it is their turn to charge at the prey. Two titles of the ranked Hunters are the Ambusher and Tracker. These titles are given to those ranked Hunters that are exceptionally skilled with certain hunting techniques.

"Scouts. These wolves are responsible for warning the Pack of dangerous territory outside the clearing, if any. Scouts are mainly wolves known by neighbouring packs and visit around often. They stay in touch with other packs and keep friendly relations. They are to report any important changes to the Alpha and Beta. These include: if a new Pack is formed;

Scouts are to find out who is the Alpha or Alphas and if the Pack is peaceful, etc.," Richie grinned ruefully and continued.

"Well, until then… anyway we eat after the Alpha and Beta eat and follow their orders. The Thetas or Elders eat before us though. An Elder is a wolf with great experience and knowledge of wolf packs. In the past they may have held such high ranks as Alpha and/or Beta. They are sometimes older members who have decided to make the pack their final resting place. An Elder's opinion is greatly respected throughout the pack, being advisor to both Alphas and Betas. They are asked to be role models to the pack, adults and cubs included, and also to visitors, showing them the Way of the Pack. They express maturity in their thoughts and actions during serious discussion or conflicts and help out where ever they can, supporting the pack through and through. The Elder lingers in the background when it comes to Pack affairs; they voice their opinions and concerns when they feel it is necessary with the utmost respect to their leaders. They just sit around all day and do nothing, sometimes the females act as Caretakers mostly meaning that they are wolves that show interest and skill in caring for weakened pack mates. They also watch over the older or ill wolves of the Pack. The Caretakers of the Pack ensure when any wolf is wounded, they recover properly not putting too much stress on their wounds. They serve as a support unit, and try to keep the pack in a healthy state. If they feel a wolf is not strong or rested enough to hunt, they are to inform the Alpha, Beta, or Hunter. Caretaking does not mean healing; it means helping to survive, to watch over and make sure one does not further hurt themselves. A Caretaker has to be stern to the wounded. Many wolves will insist they are fine. A good Caretaker needs to know what injuries are serious and what injuries can heal on their own. They need to make sure a wounded wolf, does not over exert themselves. They need to be firm in having the wolf rest… But they have enough authority and experience that well even our Alpha listens to them…You know, Danny when wolves become Thetas. They… sometimes give up their wolves –"

'What? What do you mean *give up their wolves*?"

"Well if a werewolf stops phasing for an extended period of time... say six months or so... they stop being werewolves and become normal humans again... Mostly the Thetas do this but only a very few of them... Well anyway the final member of the pack is: you the Omega. You're the last member, the butt of the pack. You eat last and basically do everything last and also you're the peace maker. Usually this is the Alpha's job but if he's not around or busy then it's your job, which means you basically break up fights between the others. Oh and you baby sit the cubs when their moms aren't around."

"Oh greeeeaaat I always wanted to eat last and break up fights," I said sarcastically.

"Hey don't worry it. It gets better in time." He looked over at me.

"Hey you okay? I mean it can't be easy to know that you're a Wolf and all but you seem to have accepted it and all so I was wondering..."

"Okay so what's Gwen's rank? Is she the Alpha? 'Because she sure acts like she is." I quickly jumped before he asked any awkward questions (Because the truth was... I had accepted it. Unbelievable I know but somehow I had accepted that this crazy messed up world of humans, vampires and werewolves did exist and I even though I couldn't still believe it, was a part of it)

Rich laughed "Nah Gwen's NO Alpha. There's an Alpha Male and an Alpha Female in every pack and they're usually mates-"

"So... who are the Alphas?"

"I thought you'd have guessed by now Danny, you're parents are." I nodded solemnly.

"So... this pack is pretty big huh?" I asked.

Richie laughed.

"Haha! Danny, the rest of the pack went on a mission somewhere I don't really know where but..."

"Whoa, whoa *rest of the pack?*" I asked.

"Well yeah. There are several other pack members too, they're just cubs like us, and some other adult wolves who are friends of Lycaon and Aniu. Right now Lycaon, Aniu and their pals make up the Alphas, Betas and Thetas of the pack…"

"Well, well what have we got here?" a menacing voice sounded behind us. I turned and saw five really buff guys standing behind me. All of them were black haired and wore shorts and the Lakers basketball jerseys.

I knew these guys' type: shallow, think they're the best in town. Beat up anyone who gets in their way… Yep, I knew 'em.

"Speak of the devil and the devil shall appear." Richie grumbled but I heard the fear in his voice.

"So who is this clown? A new recruit?" asked the guy in the middle who was tallest of the five.

"Um Trent this is Danny McMoon, the one Aniu sent us to find."

The second guy on the right laughed, "*This* guy? Ha Ha Ha Ha Ha Ha! You think this little pipsqueak is the One? The One who'll lead us to victory? Ha! He's only good for licking my…"

"Your what?" I felt my temper rise.

"If you want me to make *you* lick *my* boots just say please OK?" I smiled at him which I knew pissed him off more.

"Why you –" The guy clenched his fists.

"Shut up, Dylan! You too, Ady," the middle guy said to the first guy on his left, who also started laughing.

He loomed over me with a sneer on his face.

"So you're the son of Aniu and Lycaon, huh? The one who's gonna be Alpha? Well I've got news for you kid… I'm going to become Alpha next and you'll have to fight for your title!"

He growled and shuddered and phased. The Wolf was the darkest grey I had ever seen, even darker than Richie. The Wolf was as tall as me and had huge teeth that were as big and long as my arm!

The Wolf growled and crouched, it seemed to be waiting. Richie stepped in front of me and said:

"Look guys Danny can't change; he doesn't know how to!"

The Wolf growled again then leapt straight into the air, crashed into me and snarled in my face covering me with spit. I yelled loudly because the wolf's paws were as heavy as trucks!

Trent showed his teeth and growled… then changed back to human form and laughed then he grabbed me by my shirt collar and pulled me close to his face.

"HA… HA… The son of Aniu and Lycaon? What a joke. Listen up, kid, if you want to live… stay out of my way. Oh yeah…Welcome to the O.C… punk."

With that he laughed, got off me and stalked off with his friends. Richie ran over.

"You okay, Danny?" the poor guy seemed really worried about me.

"Yeah I'm okay. But what did he mean by I'm supposed to be Alpha?"

Richie looked uncomfortable and squirmed but he finally said:

"Danny… Well, since you're the Son of Aniu and Lycaon that kinda gives you the right to be Alpha after Lycaon."

I started laughing "HA HA HA HA… Good one bro, me the Alpha? HA… HA… that's a real good one HA… HA… Ha-ha?" I stopped when I saw his expression. He was totally serious!

I cleared my throat, "Look, man, you're not serious are you? I mean… me being Alpha?… it's just a bit tough okay and… Oh look at the time it's getting late." I quickly faked a yawn to avoid any awkward questions. Richie also seemed happy to stop talking and said:

"Hey I'll show you your room. C'mon!"

He led the way down as the sun set and into the Wolf House and up the stairs. On the first floor of the eastern wing he stopped beside a black door. A door that literally had my name on it in bold big letters carved into the wood: **DANIEL MCMOON**. I looked at the door next to the black door, saw the name and nearly jumped out of my skin. There it was in the same carved letters on my door: **GWENDOLYN DE LA ROSA**. But this door was white.

"Oh greeeeeeaaat, Gwen's next door eh?"

Richie grinned "Yeah see each floor has two rooms except for the Alpha and Beta Males and their pals. A guy and girl always occupy the rooms so you get paired with Gwen; Lee gets paired with Trisha, Ben with Sandy and so on but c'mon in and check out your room."

I stepped inside and one word came into my head.

"WHOA!"

It had a small bed, an enormous bookshelf stacked with my favourite books and novels while animals; a white and black marble elephant and lion alongside a plastic bear and a grey wolf prowled on two of the shelves, a glaring mini Cyclops shook a well-muscled arm at a single knight on another shelf while a cannon trained itself on the Cyclops. On another shelf three identical really old Ford T car models in different colours; red, green and purple were parked next to a cherry red remote controlled Ferrari three times their size. A long desk with a clock, a Swiss Army knife, a Beats headset, a model of the globe, CDs, a computer and a laptop on top of it, a dressing table with a huge mirror above it. On top of the dressing table lay a golden dagger, next to it were statues; a Chinese emperor, a William Wallace, three African Masai warriors, a single knight riding a horse and a lone Mongol horseman. You can tell I'm a history geek and medieval weapons fanatic huh? Two chairs. Two large windows a few meters in length faced each other, the southern one was just above my bed and the northern one faced it, with a large window ledge attached to both respectively. A huge wardrobe held all of my old clothes (weird). My old caps and hats hung from pegs off the western wall alongside the wigs which were souvenirs from all the plays I'd acted in during the seven years since I'd started acting. The costumes were stored in the wardrobe. My posters of motorbikes hung on the walls. A large 3D picture of wolves stared down at me from the northern wall.

The room even had a balcony that gave me an excellent view of the area around the Wolf House. I stepped out and saw Gwen on the other balcony I grinned at her but she just scowled and went back inside. I turned and went back in and saw Richie watching me.

"Dude I... err... hope you like it and uh–"

"DUDE! ARE YOU CRAZY!? THIS PLACE 'FRIGGIN ROCKS!"

He grinned. "Glad you like it."

"But, dude, one question; how did my old stuff get here?"

"Danny you were out for a day, by the way sorry about that punch but it was for your own good, so it was more than enough time for me to slip into your house. By the way your pa... err... fake parents they've moved back to Vegas; so it was easy to grab your stuff. They had left it untouched."

"Oh... um okay, dude, thanks: Night."

Richie paused at the door.

"Night, Dan. Rest up while you can cause tomorrow your training starts and believe me you're going to need every bit of rest you can get..."

"Okay. See you tomorrow."

He closed the door. I felt so tired that I just fell into bed without bothering to change and for the first time in my life I actually felt that I was at a place where I belonged. A place where I had friends and family even if they were werewolves. I felt like I had found something that everyone, poor, rich, animal, human or even the supernatural wants… a home.

Chapter 5:

Training

The only bad thing about falling asleep in a really great bed was the dream. I was running in a forest. I didn't know why but I had a feeling that I had to reach the place where I was running to. Then suddenly I was in a cave. It was dimly lit by the enormous glowing cage in the centre of it. The cage had some sort of animal inside. At a distance it looked like a bear, but as I got closer I realized it was a wolf. A giant jet black Wolf, that was as tall as me. Lycaon! Was my first thought? But the Wolf didn't make a sound and even though it looked like Lycaon I realized it wasn't.

*Daniel...*the voice was deep and spookily almost like mine. It was like two of me were speaking but the two voices were crossed. It was halfway between me normally speaking and a growl. The sound echoed around the cave. And it seemed to be coming from right behind me!

"Who... Who's there?" I spun around but no one was there.

Daniel... Daniel, help me... Then I realized it was coming from the Wolf.

"It's you. You're the voice."

The Wolf actually nodded.

Daniel you must free me.

You know when a giant Wolf asks you to let him out of a cage it's probably so you can become Wolf Chow right? But for some reason and I'm not talking about any SANE reason, I moved towards the cage and looked for the door but there wasn't one.

Free me. Now! The Wolf growled, which was about as helpful as trying to join two opposite ends of magnets together.

"I'm working on it." I groaned as I tugged at the bars. But they wouldn't budge at all.

Daniel. You must free me NOW!

"Oh yeah? I yelled feeling angry that this Wolf had done nothing to help except go 'Free me, Free me, Blah, blah, BLAH! "What do you want me to do go 'Bibbidi-Bobbidi-Boo?!Look pal I don't why I should free you. I mean why should I? You and I both know that once I set you free I'll probably wind up in your stomach!"

Daniel! Listen to me there is a great danger coming and you are the only one who can defeat it and save us all but… that is only even possible if you FREEE ME! NOW DO IT! The Wolf howled snapping it jaws inches from my face then leaped straight towards me opening its jaws to show me two rows of razor sharp teeth that would ripe me in half!

"AAAAAAAAAAAAAAAAAAAAAAAAAAAAAAAAA AAAAAAAAAAAAAAAAAAAAAAAAAAAAAAAAAAAA AAAAAAHHHHHHHHHH!" I woke up screaming. I literally jumped out of bed and I mean straight out, hit my head on the ceiling and came back down with a bump. I lay back on the bed and looked at myself: My clothes were soaked in sweat and my breath was coming out in short gasps. No bite marks, no blood and no limbs torn off, thank God!

"Phew that was close," I thought as I padded into the bathroom which had my regular brand of toothpaste and a stick of AXE deodorant. Showered and dressed, I had just reached the room door when the handle turned and the door was yanked open and I went flying out past a startled Richie, Shane, Ben, Chuck and Lee and crashed straight into the brick wall on the other side of the passage.

"Dude I'm sorry but we were just going down for breakfast and... uh you okay?" asked Ben.

"Do I even *LOOK* okay?" I asked clutching my head which hurt like... like... oh well like I'd just crashed into a brick wall okay.

"Geez sorry man but come on. We're late."

We slid down the railing and dashed into the dining room. It was a huge room with a chandelier, a round table with a place for everyone. But only Trent, Vince and Ady (which was short for Adam) and his two other cronies Vince and Carl were eating with Gwen, Trisha, and Diana while Sandy, Kelly, Ted and Sam stood to one side in a line. Then I saw the food and my stomach sat up and begged like a dog.

Piles of pancake, all kinds of meats: Mounds of sausages, Flocks of Roast Duck, Herds of mutton and what-do-you-call-deer-meat...oh yeah venison. One whole giant Christmas turkey. Stacks of ham and bacon. White hot loaves of bread fresh straight from the oven alongside jam, Nutella, maple syrup. Nests of eggs in every kind of way: Bulls eyes, poached, scrambled, you name it, it was there. Huge muffins filled with every single flavour you want. There was also a little fruit: Apples, grapes, mangoes, pineapples, peaches and oranges.

I was literally salivating at the food 'cause I had never seen so much food and rather awesomely cooked food in one place ever. I mean there was enough to feed an army and still have enough left over for the navy and air force combined!

"Whoa!" I gasped and charged the food. But a hand grabbed me from behind.

"Dude you're the Omega remember; you eat LAST!"

"WHAT! Please, PLEASE tell me you're joking."

"If I did I'd be lying' to ya. Sorry dude but that's the way it is.'"

I glanced at Trent and he grinned back and slowly and deliberately took a long bite of his drumstick which made my stomach go gaga with pain.

I had to wait until everyone had eaten then I began my meal which was only a slice of bread, a roll of bacon, an apple and two really tiny sausages .You wouldn't believe how much food a pack of eighteen werewolves could eat in just eighteen minutes!

After I ate I went outside. Richie was waiting.

"Hey, bud, okay man it's time to start your training but first I wanna see ya phase."

"Phase? Dude how'd you do that?"

"Easy. Just imagine yourself as a Wolf."

I tried it out and imaged myself as the black Wolf I'd seen in my dream… Nothing.

"Hey don't worry, keep at it you'll change sometime c'mon."

I tried again by closing my eyes. Still nothing.

"Hmm sometimes you change if you're angry or something; let me try something… Shane!" he called.

Shane ran over.

"What's up Richie?"

"Buddy, I was wondering whether you could uh help Danny out with the anger method," he said winking at him.

"No problem, Rich." And with that he hit me straight in the stomach again and again.

"Well?" he asked after he punched me enough to make me mad enough to rip him apart! "Feel anything?"

"Yeah, I suddenly have the urge to…"

"To what?" Richie and Shane asked hopefully.

"... RIP YOU IN HALF!" I yelled and ran at them.

"AAAAAAAAAAAAAAAAAAAAAAAAAAAAAAAAAAAA
AAAAAAAAAAAA" Shane yelled as I chased him around
the house. (Richie had already disappeared)

After I had caught Shane and launched him straight into
the pool, Richie came over and said,

"Well I guess you aren't changing which is weird because
usually that works on us, but the fact that it didn't work on
you is... I don't know... strange but I guess you'll change
when its time so we'll train you as a human. C'mon."

After that Rich and the others watched as I ran through an
obstacle course and lifted weights all designed to increase my
speed, strength and stamina. After that hard training again I
had to wait until the others had devoured lunch. Only then did
I have my small itsy bitsy lunch. After that I went back into
training and mind you it was hard I mean do you think that
any of you, Readers, can run around a field the size of a
football stadium five times while dodging obstacles along the
way? Anyway I trained for the rest of the day and by sunset I
was dead beat (emphasis on *dead*). I hated the thought of
eating last, so I skipped dinner even though it was a barbecue
(and I LOVE a barbecue!) and fell straight into bed.

This was the pattern for several days. At first it was tough,
I'm not gonna lie to you; but after a while I began to get used
to it. Every day, I could run further and faster. I could lift
heavier weights. I could keep running for one hour straight
without getting tired. I could feel my body getting stronger
and tougher. I looked in the mirror one day and leapt back in
surprise at the sight of my reflection: I'd always been a bit
slim and physically fit but now... I... I... had the beginnings
of a SIX PACK! My biceps were strong and firm not flabby
anymore. Yes!

I met the other members of the pack at dinner once. I
gasped in surprise when I saw them. They smiled at me and
the ladies even gave me hugs. They were my old neighbours
from Las Vegas!

"Yes, I ordered them to keep an eye on you, until you were old enough to join us again." Lycaon stood in his human form clasping my shoulder.

"And we saw you mature into a fine young Wolf," one of them put in with a smile.

"He will be a great prince, Lycaon," another added, putting a hand on my Lycaon's shoulder.

"I'd rather he would be a great son first." Aniu smiled. We all burst into laughter but my head was spinning; Prince?

One thing I'd always done was research about things I wanted to find out and now that I was supposedly a Wolf. I figured I needed to know about myself. So I started researching, everything I could find about werewolves, Lycans, lupine etc. I probably knew more than anyone in the pack about the Wolves. I studied about the effects, the moon had on us. How we would kill, how we would fight, how we hunted, pack rankings… everything.

I even started researching vampires. You know zombies right Reader? You know the mindless, insane gruesome killing machine with blood and gore dripping from its mouth bent on ripping you to pieces? Got a picture of it in your mind? If you do... then you have a pretty good idea of what a 'new' as in newly bitten vampire is like during the first few months since its transformation. As it turns out, a zombie, after a time period of about six months or a year would 'evolve' and when I say evolve, I don't mean the Pokémon type. The zombie's brain would start to develop and it would develop a kind of intelligence becoming a vampire. Even though vampires are pretty powerful on their own with cunning and speed to match.... the zombie phase of a vampire's life... is the period where it is close to being completely invincible.

A zombie will not care if you have destroyed half its body. It is bent on tearing you apart. Because of its mindless intellect, it does not feel pain; it does not feel fear or intimidation. Its brain controls it, driving it on to pass its viral curse onto others ... which is basically anything with even a drop of human blood. The only way to kill a zombie is decapitation. Fire won't work. Neither will a stake. Only if you separate brain from body do you have a dead zombie. It also has another weakness; its speed. A zombies' average speed is the pace of a walking human.

Vampires however... are a different deal. You must've heard all the legends, I mean, vampires are known almost in every culture. The Babylonians, the Ancient Greeks and Romans; the people of Africa and central Europe all have their vampires. The Indonesians have the Puntianak, India The Vampir and Ireland the Dearg-dul or red blood sucker.

I'm sure you have heard of all the myths surrounding vampires? Black capes, garlic, crosses? Yeah? All of it? It's FAKE! You wanna know the REAL vampire?

It doesn't wear a black cloak. It is not afraid of running water or garlic or crosses or priests of any kind. Look in a mirror, you'll see it's face. Neither... and I mean NEITHER is it a tragic hero, a lost soul doomed to roam the earth mourning dead girlfriends or wives that SOME legends say they are. The real vampire is an apex predator. Heart of stone. Utterly devoid of any feeling. A predator's heart. Ticking like a clock and when your time is up Reader... it kills without sentiment or hesitation.

A vampire is one of the most dangerous creatures to walk the earth. It's a super predator, using cunning and seduction to lure the victim close... and then without any hesitation will rip out your neck, fangs closing in and snapping the windpipe and jugular vein in seconds. Basically to a vampire... if you're human... you are only one thing... dinner. Normally vampires are solitary creatures but some have started to form packs of their own or 'covens' as they call them to stakeout larger territories and to have a better chance against us.

Richie and the others tried every day to get me to phase but still nothing happened.

Lycaon himself and Uncle Nathan, his Beta started to train me in a close quarter combat, training me to kill vampires. They taught me that a vampire's speed was probably its greatest asset and to be wary of it because of my inferior speed and reflexes. They taught me how to lull a vampire close and then strike, quick and clean. As a human there were limited ways I could kill a vampire. Decapitation was one. I started training with a Vietnamese war axe that Lycaon gave me. This axe was heavy but it was primarily a one handed weapon but because I had small hands I could easily wield it two handed. Alongside the axe, I had another weapon, the ornate golden dagger turned out to be a clever disguise. Beneath the gold leaf was a sharp stake. Using a stake and axe, I only had one chance to kill a vampire. If the stake didn't pierce the heart, the vampire could kill me before I could strike again. If I didn't decapitate it in one blow, I was dead. I trained with both weapons daily, becoming moderate with the dagger and slightly below with the axe. I learned that using surprise and quick reflexes was the most effective and only assets a human had against such a deadly opponent and being moderate wasn't good enough. To survive as a human in battle against one of those blood suckers it was either a quick kill or a gruesome death.

Trent and his four cronies thought that the whole thing was a joke, like I was a lost cause and every single night that blasted Wolf in my dreams kept pestering me into letting him out but the cage bars were too strong until I fell asleep one night…

Chapter 6:

Bikes and a new brother and sister

Once again I found myself outside the Wolf's cage.

"Hello again Daniel. You must free me now or you and your pack will be destroyed..."

I couldn't get why I kept pulling at the bars, I mean why would I free a humongous Wolf? But something told me that if I didn't I would regret it so I kept pulling but it still wouldn't budge.

"Daniel you Must free me because if not... Daniel... Look at me..."

I looked into the Wolf's yellow eyes and suddenly I saw a vision:

It was dark and the Wolf House was under attack! A circle of flames surrounded the house. I saw human like shapes attacking a group of Wolves... holding them back a short distance from the blazing inferno but then I saw their white skin and sharp teeth... Vampires! I also saw huge wolves that weren't attacking the vampires but were *helping them*. Then suddenly a face loomed out of the darkness. It leered at me and grabbed me; it snarled changing into a dark-silver Wolf with red/yellow eyes that looked a bit like Richie except this

Wolf wanted to kill me. It opened its huge jaws and brought them clashing together!

I woke just as Ben was coming into my room.

"Hey, Dan!"

"Ben?" I yawned. "What time is it?"

"It's Midnight. You ready? 'Cause today you get to go on patrol today with me and Sandy."

"Really? All right!" Now I was totally jazzed.

After I'd showered and changed. I met Sandy outside my door. I followed her and Ben to a huge building with no windows and several steel doors in different colours.

"Whoa! What's in here, guys?"

"Well since you can't phase your dad allowed us to use our other mode of transport today but normally we use it on trips." Said Sandy.

"Oh cool! So what is it?"

Ben led the way in: The place was huge! And right in the middle of the room was a curtained off area. Ben pulled a string and the curtain opened revealing the coolest motorbikes I'd ever seen! They weren't any particular brand but they were still awesome and all of them had a wolf's head at the head of the bikes and the headlamps were the eyes of the wolf's head. And they were of various colours, the exact colours of the wolves of the pack and each had names on them too.

"Wow! You guys get to ride these?" I yelled in excitement.

"No." Sandy said simply, and I felt a little crestfallen because I wanted to ride one of these beauties so badly it hurt.

"*We* get to ride them. You're one of us now Danny, don't forget that." Ben said with a broad smile.

"All right! But... wait, guys, we're not sixteen yet, we don't have licenses."

"That's why whenever humans look at us while we're on our bikes with our helmets we all look like we are sixteen."

"Awesome!" Now I was totally psyched up! But then a question struck me.

"But how did you get these bikes? I mean parents don't exactly give you a million bucks just to get these bikes right?"

"No we didn't buy 'em, Ben built them," Sandy said, proudly.

"No way!" I looked at him. Ben was blushing and hunching down, embarrassment evident on his face.

"It's true he built them all by hand."

Ben blushed and mumbled,

"It's nothing I just got a few parts... and put them together... It's nothing huge..."

"DUDE! Have you gone loco? I don't think anyone could have built these butt-kicking machines. You're a genius!"

"Oh um...thanks." He sort of smiled as I clapped him on the back.

"Okay so which one's mine?" I asked already imagining a really cool top-of-the-line bike.

"Um... well yours... err... is over there."

Ben said pointing at a dark shape under a tarpaulin cover. I dashed over and ripped off the cover. I was imagining trumpets and a dramatic drumbeat in my head but that suddenly vanished when I looked at the bike. It was totally... OLD! It was a rickety old bike with tires barely hanging on it and covered in rust. It didn't look like it could even make it through the door.

Ben ducked his head.

"Sorry, Dan, I fixed it up as much as I could but then Trent ordered to stop. He said you had to earn yourself a better bike. But I fixed it so you can still use it."

"Well are we going on patrol or what?" Sandy called already on her sand-brown bike which was called *Sandstorm*.

Ben climbed on his as well; a bike called *Racer*. They looked at me a little ashamed that they had those two super wheels while I had this piece of junk.

"Well," I said with a fake grin "Let's hope I earn a better bike fast. C'mon let's go."

I jumped on my bike and it made an odd creaking sound. Boy if Ben had fixed it up I wondered how it was *before*. It took five tries to get it kick started and then it needed a push to get moving. (Some of you might be wondering where the hell I'd learnt to ride a motorbike. Three words: Virtual Video games. Plus Uncle Nathan, one of my 'former neighbours' had taught me on his old TVS bike.) Ben and Sandy literally made me eat dust as we left the Wolf House and headed into the woods. Ben called out as we travelled.

"Sorry, Danny, we'll slow down a little."

Soon we were riding in a line with Ben and Sandy on either side of me and you know even though we were on patrol, Sandy and Ben turned out to be really fun and I realized that whilst most of the younger members of the pack still treated me like an outsider, Ben and Sandy had accepted me like family. I felt like I could trust them with my life. It felt like they were my own brother and sister. With teasing Ben about his lanky body and childhood memories, and Sandy screaming when Ben and I snagged a branch on her hair, and the two of them laughing as I recalled some truly mortifying and embarrassing stories about my old life, we had a great time.

We travelled all the way to the Grand Canyon which was the border of the pack's territory but there was no sign of the bloodsuckers and when we finally got back home I knew that Sandy, Ben and I were always destined to be friends.

When we got back home, we made our way to the basketball court. Yeah even though I was one of the shortest in the pack, I played a little ball. Sandy and Ben played ball too. Sandy was tall enough to be centre and an extremely good shooter. Ben was still learning but he had potential and I took it upon myself to be his coach. Normally when we played ball, it was two on one. We generally mixed it up but Ben rarely played by himself so it was usually me or Sandy who played solo.

I snagged my ball which was lying beside the hoop and tossed it to Sandy who took a shot. Nothing but net! I smiled as I walked over to my father's stereo and hit play on the CD. The High School Musical song: 'Get'cha Head in the Game' blared out. Sandy and Ben smiled too. This movie had inspired us; it was the first movie we'd ever watched together.

Sandy started bouncing the ball to the beat. I moved up to block her, she shot. I started muttering the lyrics under my breath. She grinned and started singing too. The ball bounced off the ring, Ben and I leaped for it, the ball bouncing off our fingers and landing close to Sandy. She grabbed it and went for a layup. I leaped up and hit the ball out of her hand. It bounced out of bounds. Ben took the throw in. I started blocking Sandy but she started moving, slippery as an eel. Narrowing my eyes I ran forward just as the ball was thrown. Snatching the ball I raced for the hoop. Ben blocked me. I started dribbling the ball from side to side, moving to the beat of the music and wiggling my eyebrows at Ben (a thing which I found made people either freak or laugh). Ben started laughing. We all did. It was contagious.

"Remember Benny, I'm bigger and stronger than you, but you are faster and nimbler. Use your skills little brother." I coached as the ball bounced. Ben nodded then lunged; I sidestepped and spun around him. Sandy closed in, I faked right and went left, did a layup and…. SCORE! I high-fived Sandy as I tossed the ball to Ben.

"How did you know that I would do that?"

"Your eyes." I smiled. "Always anticipate where the ball is gonna go then position yourself to steal it. But that was a good try, man." I gripped his hand, pulled him in close and clasped his head ruffling his short hair. He in return tried a sucker punch but I caught him in a head lock and started knuckle rubbing his head.

"And another thing… why don't you shoot so much?"

"'Cause I'm not good at it?"

"You aren't good at layups because you're shorter than Sandy and I. But that means you have to train yourself to shoot from greater distances such as the three point line. Alright?"

"Yeah."

"Good man." I bounced the ball over.

"Your ball."

The game continued until the score stood; nineteen to seventeen. I commented on the game all the time. "Number fourteen; Benjamin Beckett with the ball! – A beautiful layup by number eleven and soon-to-be basketball star… DANNY MCMOOOOOOOON! And… it's in! The crowd is going wild here at the Silver Moon stadium!"

I had the ball and the lead. One more shot and the game was mine. I passed it to Ben for a check. He passed it back. Immediately both of them started double teaming me. I weaved and ducked, but the defence was too strong. I held the ball looking for a shot but couldn't do anything. I held the ball behind in my hands away from my body, wondering about my options. At best I could shoot and get the rebound.

Then suddenly the ball was gone! Stolen right from my hands! But that was impossible… Sandy and Ben were right in front of me! I turned… and there was Lycaon, spinning the ball on his little finger.

"Care to make this game a little more interesting?" he smiled; I exchanged a look with Sandy and Ben. They nodded. I turned to him.

"CUBS VS WOLF!" we yelled in unison. Ben shot forward, stole the ball and passed it to me. I passed it to Sandy who was right under the hoop… SCORE!

"Kids: one... Adult: zero." I emphasized the zero as I passed the ball back to Lycaon.

The three of us grinned... for the last time during the sixty minute game. Lycaon had an aggressive style. He used his bulk and muscle to full advantage and he wasn't afraid to play rough. In fifteen minutes I supported a bruised finger while Ben was on the floor, Sandy remained untouched... for a while. We did our best to score, I played as aggressively as I could but Lycaon scored time and time again as our defence crumbled around him. And our offence ... was crushed; totally and clinically annihilated. He was like a tank and used his body to block us. Even when we shoved him we couldn't make him move at all! And he could call out any foul even when we didn't see it. Ben got called for double dribbling. Sandy was called for travelling and I was called... several times for putting my hand in his face. (Hey when you're short, they should make allowances!)

The score was... eighteen...to ten... We were exhausted... Lycaon was waaay fitter than he appeared to be. The ball was lying on the concrete floor... Lycaon and I raced for it. I reached it first and clung to it. He grabbed it too and the two of us had a very vicious and extremely ferocious tug-of-war battle over it. Lycaon was stronger, that was a fact, and his Wolf strength was enormous. He flung me about like a rag doll but I hung on grimly, nails digging into the rubber, animal like snarls rumbling from my throat as I bared my teeth (That certainly was unexpected)... No way was he going to score this time. I got bashed several times but clung on like a wildcat to the ball... until he at last called a jump off. He and I faced off. Ben was positioned just behind me while Sandy was behind him.

The ball was up and we both leapt for it. Due to his superior height and speed Lycaon reached it first. He grabbed it and went for the basket. There was nothing we could do as we watched the ball sail smoothly into the ring. I put on my hands on my knees, my breath coming out hard and fast. Ben just lay on the floor, Sandy leaned against the hoop.

Lycaon wiped his forehead. He was tired too; his breath was coming in fast. He smiled.

"Okay… how about a bet?"

We looked at him. "If you three lose… No TV for a week." His eyes glinted with mischief. I looked at him in disbelief. Ben sat bolt up. Sandy stood like a statue, eyes wide as she digested the words.

"Timeout!" I called the other two together.

"No TV for a week? He can't mean that… Can he?" Ben's eyes were wide.

I shook my head grimly.

"Sorry guys… but he means it." We all gulped at the prospect.

"What now?" Sandy asked.

I looked them straight in the eyes and thrust my fist out.

"We win."

They nodded and thrust their own fists out.

"ONE, TWO…THREE, SILVER MOON!"

We played our hearts out that half an hour. Nothing could stop us. We were driven by our cause, our goal. We were united by that cause. Nothing… and I repeat, NOTHING WAS GOING TO STAND BETWEEN US AND TV!

We pressed Lycaon hard on defense, pushed ourselves to the limit on offense. I had been trying out different moves and formations with Ben and Sandy over the weeks and now all that training paid off. We kept the ball moving, never giving him time to anticipate; sometimes passing, sometimes dribbling. We shot with precision (and sometimes at random.) Shot after shot went in until the score stood nineteen to eighteen. Lycaon had the ball.

He passed it to me. I passed it back. We crowded around forcing him to lift the ball high. I nodded at Ben. He blinked a response and circled behind, then jumped, snaking the ball from Lycaon's hands. He let out a grunt and blocked Ben. He bounce passed it to me. Lycaon switched to me. I passed it back to Ben. He was looking for an opening. The only person open was Sandy.

"Sandy, take it!" I yelled, momentarily distracting Lycaon. Sandy caught the ball but she was blocked by Lycaon who used his speed to the fullest advantage. She tried passing it to me but I was blocked too. Ben had retreated to the three point line which we counted as two points if we got a basket from there. He was our passer. He usually passed the ball and rarely shot. Sandy bounced it to me. Our luck was holding so far but for how long. If I tied the score Lycaon would have the ball... if we could score two...

I passed to Ben.

"SHOOOOOOOOT!!!!!" I screamed at him. The boy was standing there looking shell-shocked as Lycaon loomed over him.

"Sandy!" The two of us raced to screen him.

"Ben!"

He looked at me. I nodded at him and gave him a thumb up.

"Go for it little bro."

He nodded and his face became serene as he sighted and shot. The ball flew through the air and struck the backboard. Lycaon, Sandy and I watched as the ball started spinning around the hoop like a race car on a circuit. Then it stopped for a second... It was leaning... Ben's face was ashen but his eyes glimmered with excitement then shock as the ball slowly fell... inside the hoop!!!!!!

All was silent for a moment except for the ball bouncing off the cement. Then Sandy and I rushed towards Ben, hugging him and yelling.

"YES! YES! WELL DONE, BEN!" I shouted, lifting him onto my shoulders and prancing about, shouting and laughing with my little brother. Sandy was laughing as she high-fived her brother. My father was smiling and gave me a high-five as I congratulated him on his playing.

"Good game, son."

"Thanks... Dad..." I smiled up at him. He looked shocked for a second then pulled me in for a hug. Then he smiled patted my shoulder and turned to leave.

"Hey um... we were wondering..." I indicated the Beckets and myself.

"Could you show us some moves?" My father nodded smiling.

"Sure thing. Now c'mon inside, let's get some water."

Still carrying Ben on my shoulders, Sandy, my father and I headed inside... where my father promptly pushed us into the pool to 'cool off' after our victory. He wasn't laughing when Aniu did the same thing to him... and neither was she when Uncle Ned pushed *her* in and leapt in himself with a loud whoop. Soon all the older Wolves were in the pool, laughing, splashing and getting soaked to the bone.

I was happy. Looking around at the pack, yelling, laughing and splashing about in the water... I realized something... a Wolf pack isn't a gang or crew... it is a family... and this... was *my* family.

Chapter 7:

Invasion

Tomorrow's my birthday! That was my thought as I walked through the Wolf House. Once patrol and training for the day was over I decided to pay Aniu a visit, I wanted to find out the truth. I entered the cave and nearly fell because instead of Aniu, I saw a lady: who was really pretty and looked about in her thirties or early forties: Slim and fit with shoulder length black/brown hair and brown eyes.

She grinned when she saw me.

"Hello, Daniel."

"Aniu? Is that you?"

"Yes this is my human form."

"Aniu I want to know the truth. Why did you leave me with Darren and Ashley? Why was I taken away?" I wanted the truth and nothing else and I feeling Aniu could sense that.

Aniu sighed, "I always knew this day would come. Daniel, you were born during a time of danger. This danger was from 1990 to 2012. It was during this time that a great danger rose. The Time of the Vampire. It was a dangerous time for the Wolves. The vampires had come over in numbers from Europe and were at the height of their power because they had found a great store of wild wolf's bane."

"What's that?"

"The plant that every werewolf fears. The only thing that can kill us."

"What about silver bullets and fire?" I asked.

"No, those are only legends made up by humans to make them think that they stand a chance against us or more specifically the hybrids who hunted them but the truth was they would have died if it hadn't been for us and fire only affects vampires," she replied.

(Reader, ever notice that vampires are so easy to kill while it's really hard to kill a werewolf? Since there's only one thing that can kill us while there are like at least five things that can kill a vamp: Fire, Sunlight, Stakes, Decapitation and the most important and guaranteed killing machines: Us)

"But as I was saying, Daniel, it was a terrible time but hope rose when it seemed like no hope existed. A prophecy was born. In 1998 on the twelfth of August. A prophecy about the Wolf, who would be born that day who would face the greatest and most dangerous threat we would face and although he would face difficulties and sacrifices along the way... At the end of it all our fate... The fate of all werewolves... would rest on his shoulders as he faced an impossible fight and choice. And on that day *you* were born... a month earlier than expected."

Aniu continued.

"But as soon as the vampires heard these rumours, they welcomed the chance of us being wiped out and immediately set out to find and *kill* the Son of Lycaon and Aniu so you weren't safe." (Huh never knew I was *that* popular).

"We called upon two humans who were wandering nearby, in the woods, and gave you to them. So they raised you for fourteen years since you're turning fourteen this year.

Daniel, please try to understand we know how you feel but it was for your own safety."

"I... I understand Aniu... Thank you." I turned to leave my heart pounding my head filled with questions: Am I really the One in the prophecy? What is the threat that I am gonna face? But my thoughts were cut by Aniu's voice.

"Daniel... Wait..."

I turned back to Aniu.

"Daniel, you have to stop calling me 'Aniu' I am your Mother."

I thought for a minute.

"Okay but you have to stop calling me 'Daniel' everyone calls me Danny. You make me sound like a Grandfather." I retaliated

Aniu laughed. "Ha ha, I see you have something of me in you after all, not just your father even though he's very pleased about the fact... All right, Danie– Danny."

"Thanks...Mom."

She smiled but suddenly a howl sounded from the west and the smile dissolved.

"It's Lycaon. Trouble's coming."

With that we dashed from the room. Dad and the others were looking out of the windows.

"Lycaon what's going on?" Mom asked.

I looked around at the others, their faces were pale.

"What are you guys looking at?" I asked.

Ben swallowed and pointed towards the trees, at first I couldn't see anything but then suddenly there was a flash of movement and I looked into the blood red eyes of Karen Blood that glowed with thirst. She grinned up at me and then waved her hand and suddenly there were blood red eyes everywhere. Thirty vampires marched out from the trees but that wasn't all, out of the trees walked a pack of twenty five werewolves led by a huge (and when I say huge I mean bigger than Dad) dark brown almost black male. Dad growled and let out a small sharp intake of breath.

"Is that…?"

"Yes."

Dad's voice was barely a voice anymore

"It's Fenrir…And the Blood Moon Wolf Pack…"

"But that means –"

"Yeah," Gwen's voice cut in. Her face was pale.

"The invasion has begun."

Chapter 8:

A Star is born!

Dad wasted no time. He set us to work making a petrol and alcohol barrier around the perimeter of the Wolf House and then made us set fire to it creating a blazing inferno. He told us older cubs to stay inside while he led the older wolves in an attack; we would be back up.

Then Trent told all the cubs the plan: Kill every single goddamned vampire!...and also attack Fenrir's pack. He told Gwen to take the girls to cover the flanks while he led the guys in a head-on attack.

It sounded like a good plan but as you probably guessed I got the most important job ever and that was: Guard the door. Important job huh? NOT! I was given a flaming branch with the end sharpened to a deadly stake for close combat to defend myself but that was all. Then I heard a loud roar and saw the vampires charge. Fenrir's pack was just watching for now but already things were going wrong. As I watched from the doorway, the two lines collided and mayhem broke out.

Mom and Dad and the other Wolves attacked with everything they had ripping, snarling, roaring and tearing at the ones who had invaded our territory. The vampires kept coming and coming but each time they were killed or driven back. The Wolves were fighting with all the courage they could muster but there were too many vampires to fight. I heard Dad howl, Trent and the guys immediately ran full front at the chaos, phasing as they ran, the girls ran along the sidelines and attacked from the flanks.

Gwen went right for Karen and the two went down slashing and snarling. Ben and Sandy were fighting side by side with Shane, Lee, Ted, Sam and Richie. Trent, Vince, Dylan, Carl and Adam were surrounded but fighting hard. Kelly was fighting a group of vampires that were also battling Trisha and Denise who were fighting their way towards Gwen.

Then suddenly two blood red eyes lunged at me. I swung my branch and the vampire dissolved into a pile of ashes but then the other vampires noticed me, they must have thought I was human because a trio stopped fighting and ran straight at me. I swung my branch wildly and managed to set two on fire but then I found myself on the ground with a pair of blood red eyes burned into my eyes. The vampire was female with short brown and orange hair tied in a ponytail. She raised a clawed hand to my throat but a cannonball of dark silver cannoned into her.

It was Richie! He stood over me snarling at the vampire, but the vampire was now joined by six other bloodsuckers and they fell on me and Richie like rain. I swung my flaming stake while Richie attacked with his fangs and claws. Within seconds all that remained were a pile of ashes. I grinned at Rich and he phased back and grinned back but suddenly he fell back onto the ground. I rushed and knelt by his side. I saw to my horror Richie had a small plant sticking out of his chest.

"Richie! Bud, you okay?" (I know it's a stupid question but it was the first question I could think of)

"Danny... wolfs bane dart... Stupid vampire..." He groaned.

"Richie you're gonna be okay, don't worry I'll get help." I raised my head to shout for help. Suddenly Richie gripped my arm.

"N... No... Danny... I'm dying... There's no... Cure for wolfs bane... you have to fight without me... okay bro? G... Good... Good luck... Omega... I'll see you someday... on the other side..."

With that Richie closed his eyes... Then he suddenly stood up straight and strong almost like he was healed. I nearly hugged the guy but then he... he... howled the Death Song (The howl that every wolf/werewolf sings before he dies).

As his howl rose higher and higher so did he until he was standing on all fours. I felt tears form in my eyes... Then suddenly the Song was cut off abruptly... and he fell back. I couldn't hold my grief in and tears fell unashamedly down onto his broken body as I buried my face in the crook of his neck and sobbed. Silver light formed around him and dissolved into him then rose out of Richie's corpse into the sky. As I watched the light flew up towards the sky and disappeared. Then a light shone and I realized there was a new star in the sky. It was Richie!

See I'd read somewhere once that all the stars in the sky were really the spirits of dead werewolves and once a Wolf dies a new star is born from that wolf's spirit. (I know what you're thinking: What a lunatic. Doesn't this nutcase know that stars are really balls of gas? Well I don't really know what to believe but I do know something: that a star had appeared straight after Richie's death and I like to believe that his spirit is up there watching us... living forever in the stars)

"Richie? Richie! No... you can't die! Richie! No, NOOOOOOOOOOOOOOOOOOOOOOOOOOOOOOOOOOOOOO OO!!!!"

I screamed out loud, feeling something wet roll down my cheek: one of my best friends was dead. I was breathing hard, tears streaming uncontrollably down my face...

Then I heard a scream. I looked over my shoulder and saw Karen standing over Gwen who was in her human form. Gwen had several wounds on her body, her white t-shirt was soaked in blood and her jeans were torn and her face was bruised and bleeding. I looked at her and I felt mad. I'd already lost Richie I wasn't going to lose Gwen too! I was so angry that I just charged straight at Karen without the stake determined to tear her apart! I didn't care whether she killed me; at least I'd buy Gwen some time to kill her.

"KAREN!" I yelled as I charged towards her.

She looked up and smiled.

I was less than three feet away. Then I closed my eyes and leaped and in that split second the Black Wolf appeared in my head.

Daniel you have to free me! Break the cage! NOW!

I mustered up all my strength and focused it on one single thought: Protect Gwen.

I grabbed the bars and pulled and the bars broke and suddenly I felt... stronger... Faster... More alive than ever before... I opened my eyes and suddenly I could see further and better, my eye sight a thousand times sharper: I could see the faintest movement of Karen; when she shifted or twitched. I could smell the scent of the pack and also a sweet but icy cold sharp smell that burned my nose which I realized was the blood suckers.

Karen's face which had been smug changed into a look of surprise. Then I saw fear take its place. I opened my mouth (Which was longer than usual and somehow connected to my nose.) but instead of a yell or shout came a sound that I had never heard before a sound that no human could ever make: a snarl of pure rage.

I landed on all fours knocking her to the ground but she kicked me off her and with a whine I fell on the ground but I immediately jumped right back up.

"So you did it. I was right, you are the Son of Lycaon and Aniu, the Prince of Wolves and I shall be rewarded by bringing my coven your head!"

She said with a hiss through her razor sharp teeth. I tried to cuss to diss her but all that came out was a low snarl as we circled each other. Then without warning she leapt and pinned me to the ground and I felt tired and exhausted. But suddenly I called on the same energy and anger I'd felt earlier, but before I unleashed it, I said:

"Karen I just got one piece of advice: when you're going to kill someone... Kill them! Don't just stand there talking about it."

Then I unleashed my full fury on her and with a sickening crunch my teeth closed in on her throat, crushing her windpipe. The taste of a vampire was sweet but also that stench was just... Ugh! Yuck! I don't even want to describe it and five seconds later the death struggle although it hadn't been much of a struggle was over. Karen Blood was dead.

Then without warning and on instinct alone I put my feet which felt shorter and rounder (*and my nails seemed shorter and curved too*) on her body, threw my head back and let out a long howl of victory. I could feel the moon smiling on me, filling me with strength. I turned and looked down at Gwen. She looked shocked and awed. I caught her scent and it smelled of flowers. Then I heard...nothing at all.

I looked around and saw that both sides had stopped. The vampires looked afraid while the Wolves also looked uneasy and scared. I heard whispers all around but instead of growls, barks, snarls, whines and whimpers. I heard them as if they were human and I could understand them too: the slightest twitch of their ears, the way they held their tails, the way they moved and held themselves... every movement, no matter how small or discreet was a part of their wolf language.

Who's that Wolf? growled Trent.

Is that Lycaon? Vince whined.

Nah Lycaon's bigger Chuck barked.

"Wait… his scent it's the same one as…" Ben howled with excitement.

"Guys what happened?" I tried to get why they were so excited.

"DANNY!" they all howled.

"What's the matter? Why are you so excited?"

"Danny, you did it! You phased!"

"What? No I haven't."

I looked down and realized I was still on all fours and instead of hands I had black paws. I looked behind me and saw a black erect tail. I gave it an experimental wag, don't ask me how but the tail wagged. I ran back to the Wolf House and looked at my reflection and the Black Wolf stared back at me. I waved my paw. The Wolf waved its paw. I shook my head. The Wolf shook its head. I growled and made a snarling face. The Wolf growled and made a snarling face.

"Danny, I'm really glad you changed but stop admiring yourself and get your lazy tail moving! We've got bloodsuckers to kill!" yelled Shane.

"Right!" I yelped and charged into battle!

All that the vampires saw were my razor sharp fangs and flashing claws. I left a pile of ash and screams in my wake. But instead of fear I only felt exhilarated! A fierce thrill when my fangs tore into a vampire. Seeing their faces crumble with fear as I snarled in their faces! Ripping apart any vampire that dared challenge me! I may not have been much of a human, but I was BORN for this…

But sadly that's when Fenrir decided to join the battle, the Wolves charged. But even though most of the vampires were defeated, everyone, except me was bleeding and sporting cuts and bruises. This wasn't looking good.

"We should retreat we'll never hold them back!" whined Uncle Nathan. Now he was one of the toughest guys I knew and would never back down without a good reason to.

"Okay, RETREAT!" yelled Lycaon.

Suddenly everyone was running back towards the Wolf House but I knew that Fenrir's pack would catch us and tear us apart before then. Then Gwen stumbled and fell clutching her side which was bleeding heavily right into the path of the charging Wolves.

I immediately turned and started running back.

"Danny, you're going the wrong way! The door's THAT way!" Ben howled.

"Trisha! Diana!"

They turned and saw me running towards Gwen and immediately followed. We had never been friends but Gwen was their friend and I wanted to… no I needed to save Gwen for some reason I couldn't explain, so for once we were in mutual agreement.

"You two get Gwen to safety, I'll hold them off." I poured on speed, feeling my claws rake the ground in anticipation.

"Okay Danny." They yelped back.

I ran past Gwen, straight towards the approaching Wolves, snarling and growling, ready to tear apart the ones who had dared set foot on Silver Moon territory.

I looked back once and saw Gwen being lifted onto Trisha's back and the trio headed back, Diana was ensuring that Gwen didn't fall off. I faced the Wolves again, I was so mad: NOBODY INVADES MY HOME! NOBODY! I thought as I charged and I imagined my amber eyes glowing with hate but the Wolves suddenly stopped?

"Lycaon are we on time?" Fenrir growled.

"I'm not Lycaon." I growled still ready to rip my fangs into his fur.

"And I'm not gonna let you invade my home!" I yelled leaping at him but a wall of black fur slammed into me knocking me to the ground.

"Stand down, Danny." Dad snarled at me and my tail which had been erect like a flag went down as I became submissive to him. Then turning back to Fenrir he growled

"You're right on time, Brother."

"Whoa! Whoa! What? You two planned this?"

I looked at the rest of the pack who had now come back and had mystified expressions on their faces except for Mom and the older wolves.

"Of course you didn't think I'd leave my little brother to die did you nephew? Fenrir asked.

But I have to admit when I saw this young cub here running towards us with fire and hate and vengeance burning in his eyes, ready to defend his pack and home... well even though there are twenty five of us I thought we would end up as chopped liver, Fenrir gave a wolfy laugh.

"But didn't you two have a fight?" asked Ben.

"That was a rumour we spread so that the Cold Ones wouldn't be suspicious." Dad grinned.

"But they're so stupid it was hardly any trouble."

"And a good thing, too. They threatened to destroy my pack if I turned on them but now it's them who should fear. Come on!" Uncle Fenrir snarled.

And with that he and Dad gave a howl and charged. The rest of the pack and Uncle Fenrir's pack and I charged right behind them.

The vampires had been looking curiously at us while we had been talking. But luckily they didn't understand us. All they heard were growls, howls, barks and yaps.

When they saw us charging they went **batty** and when I say that, I mean they literally turned into bats and flew off into the night sky. The packs cheered and howled. I joined in, too, but deep in my heart I knew this war was far from over. Then the howls and cheering changed and stopped as Dad stood and went to stand beside me.

"Wolves of the Blood Moon pack and Silver Moon pack! On this field of battle we have not only defeated our arch enemy but my son, Daniel has phased for the first time and is now… the true Prince of The Wolves!!! My father howled.

There was silence for a while then Uncle Fenrir stepped to my other side and smiled at me.

"He does have your face Lycaon…"

Fenrir pointed his muzzle at the moon which hung above me, shining a natural spotlight on me.

Long Live Prince Daniel! Long Live the Prince!" He howled.

Howls erupted all around me.

"LONG LIVE THE PRINCE! LONG LIVE THE PRINCE! LONG LIVE THE PRINCE! LONGLIVE THE PRINCE! LONG LIVE THE PRINCE!"

Wolves were now bowing before me, even Trent and his friends though they didn't look happy about it. I felt a sense of pride build up in me. As a werewolf I was now a prince. As a human I was outcast. I belonged *here* with the Wolves not with humans. Now I was sure. The Wolves had started respecting me now and from now on they always would.

Then Gwen's face loomed in front of me.

"AAAAH" I howled jumping back.

"Hey Danny."

"Gwen. You're hurt! What are you…"

"We heal fast." She said showing me a fading cut on her shoulder. I knew it hadn't been there before the battle, but it already looked a week old.

"Oh okay."

"Danny… what you did back there to save me was really brave…"

"Ah… um… any… any Wolf would have done the same."

I stuttered ducking my head from her direct gazing, warm, melting chocolate-brown eyes and trying not to notice how fast my heart was beating and how pretty she looked in the moonlight, how the moon gave a soft silvery light to her white fur turning it pure silver and how beautiful her eyes looked, and how…

"WHOA! OUCH!"

Then the next thing I knew my paws were swept out from under me and I was on my back. Again! Gwen stood over me smirking.

"First rule of battle strategy, Danny: Never let your opponents distract you." And with that she winked and melted into the crowd.

I got up groaning and cursing and calling myself an idiot for falling for Gwen, I mean, why would *she* be interested in me of all people? I mean she was like one of the coolest people I knew and me… well It was just me… when a wet nose touched my shoulder I looked into the silver grey eyes of Mom.

"Mom we won!"

"I know Danny but you know as well as I do that this won't be the last battle we face."

"You mean…"

"Yes, Danny." Dad's voice came from my right.

I hadn't heard him join us and now we stood in a triangle. He looked up; I followed his gaze and looked at the full silver moon. That's when I realized something. The moon was shining directly above us. It was midnight. It was my birthday. I had just turned fourteen.

"This war… has only just begun…"

TO BE CONTINUED…